Daisy May

Roaring Good Reads will fire the imagination of all young readers – from short stories for children just starting to read on their own, to first chapter books and short novels for confident young readers.

Daisy May

JEAN URE

illustrated by
Karen Donnelly

HarperCollins *Children's Books*

For Jessica West, whose dad was once my editor

First published in Great Britain by HarperCollins *Children's books* in 2002
HarperCollins *Children's Books* is a division of HarperCollins *Publishers* Ltd,
77-85 Fulham Palace Road, Hammersmith, London W6 8JB

The HarperCollins *Children's Books* website address is
www.harpercollinschildrensbooks.co.uk

7

Text © Jean Ure 2002
Illustrations © Karen Donnelly 2002

ISBN-13 978 0 00 713369 7
ISBN-10 0 00 713369 3

The author asserts the moral right to be
identified as the author of this work.

Printed and Lound in England by
Clays ltd, St Ives plc

chapter one

Daisy May was a foundling. She was found one May morning by a farmer who was ploughing his field.

"Well, blow me down!" said the farmer. "What is this, a-lying in the grass?"

He peered closer and saw that it was a small pink bundle of baby, wrapped in a shawl. The farmer scratched his head and wondered what to do with it. In the end he picked it up and carried it back home, thinking that perhaps his wife might have some suggestions to make. But his wife took one look and cried, "Get rid of it!"

The farmer's wife already had six children of her own; she didn't want another one.

Nobody wanted poor Daisy. Not the farmer's wife, not the farmer's sister, not his aunt or his cousin or his next-door neighbour. Not the village schoolteacher, not the choirmaster, not even the parson. So the farmer gave the bundle to a passing carter, who took it up to

London and left it on the steps of a foundling hospital, with a note pinned to the shawl:

FOUND IN A DAISY FIELD.

They called the bundle Daisy May. Daisy because of the daisy field; May because that was the month in which she was found. For the next ten years the Foundling Hospital was where Daisy lived.

It wasn't her home. Home is a place where you are loved and wanted. A place that is warm and safe.

The Foundling Hospital was hardly ever warm, except at the height of summer, and then it was too hot. It wasn't very safe, cither. The little ones were bullied by the big ones, and the big ones were bullied by the grown-ups. And nobody was loved or wanted. Who would love a foundling? Foundlings were nothing but a nuisance.

The people who were supposed to look after them were cruel and unfeeling. They handed out harsh punishments, for the least little thing. They also, sometimes, stole the children's food. As a result, the foundlings were always small and thin. They were always covered in scabs and bruises, they always cowered if anyone lifted a hand. They were dressed in rags and were always dirty (except on a Sunday). Their hair was full of lice. No wonder people turned up their noses as they passed by. No wonder mothers in the street shielded their children's eyes.

"Don't look, darling! Those are foundlings."

One winter's morning when she was six years old, Daisy's hands became so numb with cold that she dropped a plate and broke it.

As a punishment she was soundly smacked and sent outside to stand in the yard. She stood for the rest of the day, shaking and shivering, her face blotched with tears.

That was the first time Daisy was cruelly punished. But not the last. Now that she was six years old she was smacked and beaten regularly, like all the others. In time she grew used to it. She thought it was just something that happened to children. Something that grown-ups did. She didn't know about mothers and fathers and families.

One day when the foundlings were being marched to church, two by two in their Sunday best, Daisy saw an amazing sight. A little girl of about her own age, walking with a lady and gentleman, suddenly slipped on the cobbled street and went sprawling to the ground. The little girl immediately burst into loud sobs. Daisy held her breath. She waited for either the lady or the gentleman to cuff the little girl round the head and tell her to "Stop that racket!" Instead, to her astonishment, the gentleman helped the little girl to her feet and the lady brought out a handkerchief to mop up her tears. Not even when it was discovered that she had torn a great hole in one of her stockings did they hit her.

Daisy couldn't believe it! She turned to Ermentrude, the big girl who was walking by her side.

"Why don't they beat her?" she said.

"They're her mother and father," said Ermentrude. The way Ermentrude said the words they sounded like *muvver* and *farver*, so naturally that was what Daisy thought they were. "Muvvers and farvers don't beat their children."

"Why not?" said Daisy.

"'Cos they loves 'em," said Ermentrude. Being a grown girl of almost nine, she knew about these things. "You're too young," she said to Daisy. "You ain't got no idea what goes on in the world."

"I can learn!" said Daisy.

Even at six years old, Daisy was determined to learn everything she could. She had already been taught how to sew, and how to scrub floors, and how to wash dishes. One day, when she was a little older, she would be taught her letters – her ABC – and how to write her name. She would be taught simple sums, such as two and two are four, and twice five is ten. But she wanted to learn other things, as well. She wanted to learn about mothers and fathers, and what went on in the world.

"I keep my eyes open, I do," she said.

Ermentrude just sniffed. What made Daisy

think *she* was so special? She was no different from the rest of them!

That night, Daisy had a dream. She dreamt that she was like the little girl in the street with the kind lady and gentleman who were her mother and father. She kept falling over, and they kept picking her up. The lady kept kissing her, the gentleman kept hugging her. It was lovely while it lasted, but then she woke up and the dream disappeared. She didn't have a mother and father. She was still in the Foundling Hospital.

Next Sunday she saw the little girl again, with the lady and the gentleman. This time there was a little boy as well.

"They're what's known as a *fam'ly*," said Ermentrude.

"Why doesn't everyone have fam'lies?" said Daisy.

Ermentrude wrinkled her brow. Why *didn't* everyone have families?

" 'Cos not everyone can afford 'em," she said. "I've got one, o' course."

"*You*?" said Daisy.

"'Course I have! They'll come an' find me one day. I was stolen from 'em, see, when I was a baby. I 'spect they're looking for me, even now."

Daisy thought about this. She decided that she would have a family, too. Her father would be a gentleman in a top hat who worked at a very important job in the City, and her mother would be… a famous actress!

14

She told Ermentrude about them, but Ermentrude grew rather cross.

"That's just lies!" she said. "You don't have any *fam'ly*."

"I do, too!" cried Daisy.

"Oh, really?" Ermentrude planted her hands on her hips. "In that case," she said, "where are they?"

"I don't know," said Daisy tearfully. "I lost 'em!"

"*Lost 'em?*"

"I went for a walk in a field an' I got lost !"

"You didn't get *lost*," said Ermentrude. "You was *abandoned*. Your muvver didn't want you."

"She did so!" wept Daisy. "She wrapped me in her shawl!" Daisy's shawl was her most treasured possession. Surely her mother must have loved her, to have wrapped her in a shawl?

15

But Ermentrude said no. "They always do that."

The truth was, Ermentrude was a little bit jealous. Ermentrude had

not come wrapped in a shawl; she had been left in an old and dirty orange crate.

"It's about time you stopped this silly daydreaming," she said to Daisy, in scolding tones. "It won't do you no good. We can't *all* have fam'lies."

Daisy drooped. She knew that Ermentrude was right: Daisy hadn't been lost, she had been abandoned. Nobody wanted her. Nobody was going to come looking for her. She would have to find something else to dream about.

Every Sunday when the foundlings went to church, (they were made to sit right at the back, well away from the rest of the congregation) a crocodile of young ladies went marching in ahead of them. They came from the Dobell Academy, just around the corner in the square.

The Dobell Academy was very superior. It was for the daughters of gentlemen. Even though the foundlings had been told repeatedly that it was rude to stare, they couldn't help shooting little glances as the young ladies swept past. The young ladies were all dressed up in silks and satins, clutching their prayer books in gloved hands and chattering to one another in their high-pitched voices, like the twittering of birds. They never even noticed the small pinched faces of the foundlings.

Daisy began to dream that one day *she* would dress in silks and satins. She would chatter in a high, bright voice. She would be a young lady!

She didn't tell Ermentrude, because she knew what Ermentrude would say.

"Just stop being so silly!"

Daisy hugged her daydreams to herself.

*   *

In the year 1887, two exciting events occurred. One was Queen Victoria's Golden Jubilee, when all of London took to the streets to cry, "God bless the Queen!" Even the foundlings were given special jubilee mugs, and little paper flags to wave.

The other event was Daisy's birthday. She was ten years old! A big age. She didn't have a birthday party, of course; foundlings never had birthday parties. In any case, no one knew for sure when Daisy's birthday was. The hospital had decided that it was 10th May, which seemed as good a date as any other.

Nobody wished her "Happy Birthday". Ermentrude, who might have done, was no longer there. She had disappeared when she was just a year older than Daisy. Daisy had this dream that Ermentrude's family had finally come looking for her, but another girl, Ellen, said that was rubbish.

"She never 'ad no fam'ly! She went off to be a kitchen maid. You will, too, soon as you're old enough."

"I'm not goin' to be a *maid*!" cried Daisy. But Ellen said that she would have no choice in the matter.

"You're no different from the rest of us – you have to go where you're sent."

It seemed that Ellen was right, for that very same morning – the morning of her birthday – Daisy was called in to the Principal's office. Two ladies were waiting to see her. They were the Misses Winter, who ran the Dobell Academy. They walked to church with the young ladies every Sunday morning. And now they had come to see Daisy.

Daisy didn't know whether to be scared (in case she had done something wrong) or excited (in case something good might be going to happen). She bobbed a curtsey, as she had been taught, and stood with her hands clasped before her and her eyes meekly cast down, as a foundling should. But she couldn't resist the odd little peek from under her lashes.

Both ladies examined her. Daisy could feel their eyes travelling up and down, taking in the details. One of the ladies, who was called Miss Gertrude, was tall and lean and rather grim. The other, Miss Fanny, was shorter and rounder and softer.

It was Miss Fanny who spoke first.

"Well, sister? What do you think?"

"The *hair*," said Miss Gertrude. She shuddered. "So vulgar!"

Daisy had never heard her hair described as vulgar before! It was true that it was rather bright. Sometimes the big boys teased her and called her Flaming Carrots or Ripe Tomato. But she had never known that it was *vulgar*.

"Oh! Well. As to that, you know," said Miss Fanny, "it will be hidden beneath her cap."

"It will need to be," said Miss Gertrude. A ripple of revulsion ran through her. "There is something unspeakably *common* about the colour red."

"But apart from that?" pleaded Miss Fanny. "Do you not think she would do?"

Daisy risked a quick glance upwards and

met Miss Gertrude's eyes, boring into her.

"She will need to be a great deal less forward!" snapped Miss Gertrude.

Daisy instantly dropped her gaze back to the floor.

"She would be more of an adornment than our poor Lottie," ventured Miss Fanny.

"We are not looking for an *adornment*, sister! We are looking for a *maid*."

So a maid is what Daisy became. As Ellen had said, Daisy was no different from the rest of them – she had to go where she was sent.

"But I'm not goin' to be a maid for ever!" vowed Daisy.

Chapter two

It was Miss Fanny who escorted Daisy across the square to the Academy. Miss Gertrude had gone on ahead, and Daisy was glad of that for Miss Gertrude frightened her. Miss Fanny was more friendly, and a little bit flustery. She chattered nonstop all the way across the square.

"Daisy May," she said. "A pretty name! And very suitable, for one in your position. In French, you know, the word for a daisy is *marguerite*. But that would not do at all! It would be far too refined. People of the lower orders," said Miss Fanny, kindly, "should never attempt to ape the ways of their betters. Do you know what ape means?"

Daisy was always eager to learn. She shook her head and said, "No, ma'am."

"It means to *copy*," said Miss Fanny. "You must never try to copy. Remember that, Daisy! Be a good girl, and do as you are told. Work hard, say your prayers, and do not get ideas above your station."

It was very important not to get ideas above your station. Getting ideas above your station meant giving yourself airs and graces and pretending that you were as good as those above you.

"Be content with your lot," urged Miss Fanny. "That way you will be happy."

Daisy promised to do her best. But nothing could stop her daydreaming. One day she was going to wear silks and satins. One day she was going to be a lady! In the meantime, she stored up the little crumb of knowledge that Miss Fanny had given her.

"In French," she said, "my name is *Marguerite*…"

To begin with, even though she hadn't wanted to become a maid, Daisy couldn't help feeling a little bit proud. Out of all the girls in the Foundling Hospital, she was the one to have been chosen. She could have been sent anywhere, but here she was, at the Academy, with all the young ladies!

She was given a new dress to wear, a black one, with a white pinafore to go over the top, and a white cap, called a mobcap, which looked a bit like a frilly chamber pot without a handle. (The cap was to keep her hair tucked away, so that it should not offend Miss Gertrude.) Best of all, she had a room of her own, up in the attic. It was not much larger than a broom cupboard, and there was not very much in it. Just a narrow bed, a small table with a wobbly leg, a chair with a broken back and a bit of frayed rug on the floor – but it was hers.

The first time in all her life that she had not had to sleep in a dormitory with rows of others!

There was another attic room next door to Daisy's. This one belonged to Lottie. Lottie was a big girl of twelve. She was not very clever, and she was not very pretty, poor Lottie. Her hands were red and chapped from all the washing-up she had to do, her hair was greasy and her chin was covered in spots. Daisy felt sorry for her. She never imagined that one day *her* hands might be red and chapped, and *her* hair all greasy, and *her* chin covered in spots.

"You are so pretty," sighed Lottie.

"Miss Gertrude said I must try to be less forward," said Daisy.

Lottie said that Miss Gertrude was probably jealous, because of Daisy being so pretty. Lottie wasn't jealous. She was sweet and gentle, and had the kindest heart. There were times when she could be maddeningly slow, and maddeningly clumsy, and then Daisy, being naturally very quick and bright, would grow impatient. But she always reminded herself that Lottie couldn't help it. Lottie was a dear! Also, Daisy knew that Lottie looked up to her, even though Daisy was only ten years old. It made Daisy try her hardest to be worthy of such admiration.

For the first few weeks of her new life, Daisy kept telling herself how lucky she was. She had a room of her own and a new black dress. Lottie was the best friend in the whole wide world, and she was living under the same roof as the young ladies. Surely, now, she would be able to make her dream come true?

But the weeks turned into months, and Daisy's dream seemed as far away as ever. She tried so hard to better herself! But the young ladies continued to look right through her as if she did not exist. They certainly never spoke to her, and Daisy, of course, was not allowed to speak to them. She was not even allowed to watch them! Miss Gertrude discovered her one day, standing at the half-open door of the drawing room as a dancing lesson was in progress. Miss Gertrude was very angry. She yanked Daisy away by her ear, and smacked her round the head, quite hard, and asked her how she dared to be so impertinent.

"What do you think you are doing, gawping

like that? Get about your business! Have you no work to do?"

Daisy had lots of work to do. She never stopped. She worked from early in the morning till late at night. These were just some of the tasks she had to perform: she carried hot water upstairs for the young ladies; she swept out the yard; she scrubbed the front step; she polished the front doorknocker; she peeled potatoes;

she took out the rubbish; she washed the dishes; she dusted and she polished; she brushed the stairs; she tidied the schoolroom; she ran errands for Miss Fanny; she ran errands for Cook; she scrubbed and scoured the kitchen ready for the next day. Only when the last greasy, grimy morsel had been scraped from the last greasy grimy pot, and the pot hung all bright and shining from its hook on the wall, was she free at last to go to her room.

The attic was like an oven in the midsummer heat. While the young ladies slept sweetly in their flower-scented rooms, Daisy tossed and turned on her narrow bed. Her legs ached, her feet throbbed, and her hands were already starting to grow red and chapped, like Lottie's. How could she ever become a lady, with hands like that?

One day, when she was tidying up the schoolroom, she came across an old slate which had fallen behind a cupboard. Daisy's heart beat a loud tattoo against her ribcage. What if she took the slate for herself? Who would ever know? It had obviously been behind the cupboard for a long time, for it was covered in dust.

Before she could lose courage, Daisy stuffed the slate into the pocket of her dress, together with a piece of chalk. Then she ran all the way upstairs to the attics and secreted both slate and chalk beneath her mattress, before scampering back down to get on with the sweeping and dusting.

She could hardly wait for the day to be over! She was so eager to get to her slate. She had been taught her alphabet in the Foundling

Hospital, and how to write her name, but not very much else. She was terrified of forgetting what little she knew. Now she could practise.

Lottie perched on the end of Daisy's bed and watched, wide-eyed, with her thumb in her mouth, as Daisy made marks with her piece of chalk. Poor Lottie had never progressed beyond the first three letters of the alphabet.

"The cat sat on the mat," wrote Daisy. "The dog sat on the log."

She showed it to Lottie, who shook her head in silent wonder.

"Now I'll write your name – look! LOTTIE. What's your other name?"

Lottie took her thumb out of her mouth. "Ain't got no other name."

"No other name at *all*?" said Daisy.

"Not as far's I know," said Lottie.

Daisy nodded, wisely. "That's 'cos you've got no fam'ly," she said. "I've got a fam'ly! I've got a father and I've got a mother." Daisy had learnt by now that it wasn't *farver* and *muvver*. She listened, and she picked things up. "My father," she told Lottie, "is very rich, and my mother is very beautiful. My mother is French," she added. "I was stolen from her when I was a baby."

She knew it wasn't true; but it was such a lovely fairy tale! And Lottie was so trusting she believed every word of it. Lottie wanted to know more. She especially wanted to know about Daisy's beautiful mother.

"Will she ever find you again?"

"Maybe," said Daisy. "One day. When I'm famous."

Lottie gasped. "You're goin' to be *famous*?"

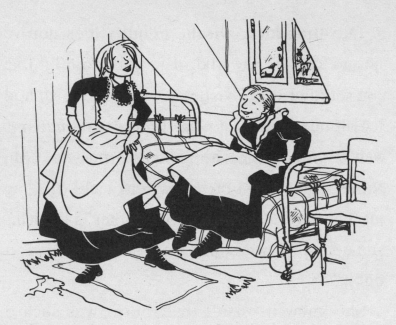

"I'm going to be a famous actress," said Daisy.

Lottie's eyes grew round as soup plates. Daisy was rather surprised, herself. But now that she had thought of it, she realised that it was true... she *was* going to be an actress!

"I shall have to have a different name, of course. I shall call myself Marguerite. Marguerite May, the toast of the town!" Daisy gave a little twirl, in the middle of the attic. "And I shall wear silk gowns," she said, "and you shall wear my cast-offs."

Every night for a week Daisy practised writing on her slate. She wrote her new name – "Margreet May". She knew how to spell May all right because she had learnt it in the Foundling Hospital, but she had no idea how to spell Marguerite.

"It's French," she explained to Lottie. "It means Daisy."

She was so busy wondering how she could find out the correct spelling that one night she became careless and forgot to hide her slate under the mattress before she went to sleep.

Next day she was called in to Miss Gertrude's private room, and there on the table was – the slate! All filled up with Daisy's writing.

Miss Gertrude picked the slate up and thrust it into Daisy's face.

"You are a thief!" screamed Miss Gertrude. "A low, common *thief*!"

She made Daisy hold out her hands while she hit them with a ruler. Then she took her outside and locked her in the coal cellar.

It was dark, down in the cellar, and there were rats. Daisy could hear them scurrying about, their claws making little scritching noises on the cellar floor. After a while they grew bold and started to run over her feet, which frightened Daisy terribly.

She screamed and screamed, but nobody came to help her. It was ten o'clock at night when at last Miss Fanny unlocked the door and told her that she could come out. Daisy was trembling so violently she could hardly walk back up the steps. Her face was grimy with coal dust and had great streaks down it where the tears had tumbled.

"Oh, my!" said Miss Fanny. "What a state you have got yourself into! But it was a wicked thing you did, Daisy! A very wicked thing. This time you have been let off lightly. But be sure not to do it again, for next time I cannot answer for the consequences. Now go to your room and pray to the Lord to be forgiven."

Upstairs, in the hot little attic, kind Lottie sponged Daisy's coal-blackened face and wrapped her poor torn hands with a piece of cloth.

"I got you some supper," she said. "Look!"

From the pocket of her apron she brought out a chunk of dry  bread and a hunk of yellow cheese.

Daisy hesitated. She would have dearly loved to take it! But she knew that the bread and cheese must have been Lottie's own supper. Cook would never have let her take extra for Daisy. Not when Daisy was in such terrible disgrace.

"S'all right," said Lottie. "You can 'ave it. I ain't 'ungry!"

But Lottie was always hungry. The scraps they were given were never enough to fill her up.

"We'll share," said Daisy; so Lottie sat on the end of the bed and they munched the bread and cheese together.

Daisy felt a bit better after that. Her hands still hurt, but at least she had stopped trembling. The worst thing was, she didn't have her slate any more.

"Don't you go worryin' 'bout no stupid slate." Lottie said it fiercely. "Slate ain't worth gettin' into trouble for."

Fresh tears went trickling down Daisy's cheek. She knew that Lottie was right, for next time the punishment would surely be even worse. (If anything worse than the coal cellar could be imagined.)

"But what's to become of me if I forget my letters?" wept Daisy.

"Letters ain't important," said Lottie. "Look at me! I done all right wiv'out 'em."

She was trying so hard to be a comfort, but

her words only brought a great despair to Daisy's heart. How could she ever hope to be a lady if she forgot her letters?

When Lottie had crept back to her own bed, Daisy lay down and tried to sleep. For a long time sleep wouldn't come. She tried counting sheep, but that didn't work. Sheep were too boring. They couldn't take away the pain in her hands, or the ache in her heart. So then she tried reciting her name. Her *new* name: Marguerite May, the toast of the town!

After a while, Daisy's eyes began to close. She forgot her throbbing hands. She forgot her aching heart. She was Marguerite May! Toast of the t… o… w… n…

Daisy had fallen fast asleep. And that was the night when it happened. The most extraordinary thing!

Chapter three

Daisy was in the middle of the most wonderful dream. She was Marguerite May, wearing a red silk dress and a hat with ostrich plumes. She was on stage, taking curtain call after curtain call. The audience were clapping and cheering, tossing flowers at her feet, calling out her name. And amongst them, cheering and clapping along with the rest, was none other than... Miss Gertrude!

Daisy never knew what woke her up. Maybe it was the loudness of the applause.

Or maybe drunken revellers in the square outside. Whatever it was, it made her jump up in bed with a start.

She saw the old lady immediately. She was sitting on Daisy's chair with the broken back. Daisy was dreadfully scared! She thought it must be Miss Gertrude, come upstairs to beat her. But she realised very quickly that it was not. This old lady was far older than Miss Gertrude. Her hair was soft and snowy white, and her eyes were sunk deep into their sockets. For all that, she was an extremely beautiful old lady. Very tiny and fragile, like a delicate piece of porcelain.

Daisy held her breath. Was she still dreaming without knowing it? Or was there truly an old lady sitting in her chair?

She saw that the old lady had a book in her lap. A scrapbook of some kind. She was turning the pages, stopping occasionally to smile or shake her head, as if reliving memories. She seemed not to be aware of Daisy. Could she perhaps be ... a *ghost*?

Daisy had never seen a ghost before. She knew that there were such things, for the big girls at the Foundling Hospital had sometimes told stories of them. Daisy had always been scared and pulled the covers over her head, but she was not in the least bit scared now! Now that she knew it was not Miss Gertrude. She had the feeling that the old lady meant her no harm. This was not someone who would cuff her round the head and throw her down into the cellar.

For the longest time, Daisy sat scrunched up in bed, with her knees hugged to her chin, small as a mouse, while the old lady leafed through her scrapbook. And then – the strangest thing! The old lady stretched out a finger to touch something on the page. Her gaze lingered for a moment, then she lifted her head and, looking straight at Daisy – or so it seemed – she smiled and said, "Be strong, my child! The fight is not yet over."

Even as the words were spoken, the old lady faded away. One minute she was there – and the next she was gone. Daisy sprang out of bed and ran to the chair. She felt the seat, but it was not even warm. Had she *really* seen an old lady? Or had she just imagined it? She was far too excited to go back to sleep! She longed to run into the next-door attic room and wake Lottie, but she knew that would not be fair. She would have to contain herself until the morning.

But even in the morning she was not able to tell Lottie. While Daisy was toiling up the stairs with buckets of hot water, Lottie was in the kitchen helping Cook with the breakfast; while Daisy was scrubbing the front step, Lottie was out

running errands; while Daisy was
peeling potatoes, Lottie
was turning out
the drawing room.
And so it went on,
the whole day.

The only time
they were together – but then Cook was there –
was for breakfast and the midday meal. Bread
and marge for breakfast, with a mug of tea; a
bowl of watery soup and the remains of
yesterday's lamb stew for lunch. Fastidious
Daisy picked out all the gristle and Cook said
she was "a little madam", giving herself airs.
Daisy, being forward, said that Cook might eat
her gristle if she wanted, whereupon Cook
smacked her with a ladle and told her to mind
her manners.

"And stop aping yer betters! What's with all this la-di-da talk?"

"I can talk as I like," said Daisy.

"Not in front of me, yer can't," said Cook, and she leaned across the table and boxed Daisy soundly round the ears.

Daisy tilted her chin. Cook could box her ears as much as she liked! Daisy was going to be a lady. She had been listening, and she had been learning. She was going to talk proper! And she wasn't eating gristle for anyone. She wasn't telling Lottie about the old lady, either, not in front of Cook. Cook would only go running to Miss Gertrude, and then it would be the coal cellar again, for Miss Gertrude certainly wouldn't tolerate the idea of having a ghost in the house.

All day long, Daisy hugged her secret. And then at last it was evening! The final pan had been scrubbed and scoured and hung on its hook, and in her usual grudging tones, Cook said that Daisy might go.

Up the back stairs she raced, two at a time, to the attic. Lottie arrived, rather more slowly, a few minutes later. Lottie never ran if she could help it.

"Oh! I've been so longing to tell you!" cried Daisy. In her excitement she seized hold of lumbering Lottie and pulled her up the last few steps. "You will never guess what... I have seen a ghost!"

Lottie's face lost its usual hectic redness and turned very pale.

"A g-ghost?" stammered Lottie.

"Yes! In my room – last night!" And Daisy gabbled it all out, about the old lady sitting on her chair.

"She was looking at a book, with pictures. I think they may have been *photographs*. And oh, Lottie! She was such a charming old lady. But dressed *so* peculiar!"

"P-peculiar how?" said Lottie.

"She was *showing her legs*!"

Daisy had scarcely noticed it at the time. It was only afterwards, looking back, that it had struck her. The old lady's dress had ended *just above the knee*. But it had not been torn! It had obviously been made that way.

There was a silence.

"I ain't never heard of no old lady ghosts showin' their legs," said Lottie.

"N-no." Daisy had to admit that she hadn't either. "But I'm sure it wasn't a dream, for she *spoke* to me. She said to be strong, for the fight was not yet over."

Lottie crinkled her brow. "What's that s'posed to mean?"

Daisy had been puzzling over it all night. "I think what it means," she said, "it means that I must not let anyone stop me... mainly Miss Gertrude," she added.

"Aow!" Lottie let out a great squawk and wrung her hands. "I 'ope you ain't goin' to go upsettin' 'er no more!"

"I shall do my best not to," said Daisy, "but if I do – well!" She tossed her head with its mass of red hair. (Which *would* keep peeping out of her cap, no matter how much she tucked it away.) "That would be just too bad," said Daisy.

"But the coal cellar!" wailed Lottie.

Lottie had been very scared when Cook had told her that Daisy had been locked in the coal cellar. She had had visions of Daisy being eaten alive by monstrous great rats. She had thought she might never see her again.

"I don't want to lose yer!" wept Lottie. "I dunno what I'd do if I was to be left all on me own!"

Daisy took Lottie's poor red hands in hers.

"It will be all right, Lottie. You'll see!"

"But the coal cellar!" sobbed Lottie.

"I must just be strong, that's all. So long as I'm strong, then one day my dreams will come true. And when *my* dreams come true, then so will yours! For when I am a famous actress," said Daisy, "you shall be my dresser and help look after me."

Lottie's face lit up.

"Really and truly? You ain't just sayin' it?"

"Really and truly," said Daisy. "That is a promise!"

Chapter four

Now it was winter. Windows frosted over and water set to solid ice. Upstairs in the attics the very air itself was frozen. Daisy could see her breath curling and billowing into the mist. It was so cold that on some days she and Lottie crept together into the same narrow bed, their arms wrapped round each other for warmth. It

was not so very much warmer downstairs in the young ladies' dormitories, but at least the young ladies had thick covers to pull over themselves. They had cloaks they could huddle under, and fur muffs to tuck their hands into. Daisy and Lottie huddled and shivered the whole night through. To keep their spirits up, Daisy would tell tales of how it was going to be when she was a lady, and a famous actress.

"I shall have me own horse and c—" Daisy stopped. She was trying *so* hard to sound like a young lady. "My own horse and carriage," she said. "And a coachman, to drive me."

"A coachman!" breathed Lottie.

"Yes," Daisy nodded. "I shall call him James, and he will call me Madam, and I shall have a house with crimson wallpaper, both upstairs and down. There will be rugs on the floor, and

I shall always have wax candles. The most expensive ones!"

"What colour will the rugs be?" asked Lottie. She was always hungry for all the details.

"All colours! Reds and greens, and blues, and yellow... different colours for all the different rooms. There will be a great many rooms."

"How many?"

"Dozens," said Daisy. "I shall have two drawing rooms, one for best, and one for everyday. And a dining room, a big one, for all the supper parties I shall give. And bedroom after bedroom! For my house guests, you know."

Lottie nodded breathlessly.

"And, oh, Lottie, I shall have a ballroom! A grand ballroom with a crystal chandelier."

"Crystal!" Lottie clasped her hands ecstatically.

"And lemon silk curtains, all looped up. And of course there will be maidservants to keep the place clean and to fetch and carry."

"I'll fetch and carry!" said Lottie, but Daisy said no. She said that Lottie was going to be her dresser.

"You will come with me to the theatre and look after my costumes. It will be your job to make sure they are all cleaned and pressed, ready to wear. That is what a dresser does."

Lottie shook her head in wonderment. Daisy knew so much! How did she come by all this knowledge?

"I look and I listen," said Daisy. "That way, I learn."

In spite of Miss Gertrude having smacked her round the head, Daisy took every opportunity she could to watch the young ladies. She watched them having deportment lessons, learning how to move gracefully. They must not scurry or scamper, as Daisy had to if she wanted to get her housework done and not have her ears boxed by Cook. They certainly mustn't thump on leaden feet as poor ungainly Lottie did. Instead, they must glide like swans across the room, with books on their heads to make sure they didn't wobble.

Daisy didn't have any books, but she practised with a cracked plate that Cook had thrown out with the rubbish, and now she, too, could glide like a swan.

She could talk like the young ladies, as well! She was getting better and better at it. She had heard them at their elocution lessons. "How now, brown cow," in their clear, high voices. Lottie giggled when Daisy imitated them.

"Now you try," said Daisy, but Lottie was bashful and shook her head, and said that Daisy had better not let Miss Gertrude hear her talking like that.

Daisy squawked, "Lor, no, ma'am! Beggin' yer parding, ma'am!" and bobbed a little curtsey, which made Lottie start giggling again.

It took a great deal to squash Daisy's high spirits. No matter how many times Cook let fly with her ladle, or Miss Gertrude smacked her with a ruler, Daisy always came bouncing back. So when Lottie found her in tears one day, she knew something serious must have happened.

"What is it?" cried Lottie in alarm.

"My hands!" sobbed Daisy.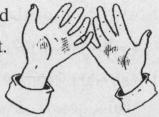
"Look at them!" She held
them out for Lottie to inspect.
Daisy's hands were now as
red and sore and cracked
as Lottie's. "How can I be an actress," wailed
Daisy, "with hands like this?"

Lottie didn't know what to say. Lottie's hands
had been red and sore for so long she had almost
forgotten they had ever been anything else. Lily-
white hands were for ladies. And in spite of her
wonderful daydreams, Daisy was only a humble
skivvy, the same as Lottie.

"Don't you go worryin' bout no 'ands," said
Lottie. "They ain't as bad as all that."

Daisy refused to be comforted. "They're
hateful!" she wept.

But it never took Daisy long to recover. That very same evening, she was happy again.

"Look!" she said. "See what I've got!"

Lottie gaped. From beneath a loose floorboard, Daisy had produced a little pot of... *goo*.

"What is it?" whispered Lottie.

"Goose fat!"

Goose fat from the kitchen, from the goose that Miss Gertrude and Miss Fanny had had for Sunday dinner.

"I am going to rub in a little every night," said Daisy. "You can have some, if you like," she added. But Lottie backed away in terror. She didn't want anything to do with it!

"You'll catch it," she said. "You'll catch it somethin' awful if Miss Gertrude finds out!"

"Well, she won't," said Daisy, putting the pot back beneath the floorboard.

But Miss Gertrude did. She was making one of her inspections of the attics, just to check that neither Lottie nor Daisy was becoming too comfortable or too cosy, or had somehow managed to find extra covers to go on their beds, when she noticed that one of the floorboards in Daisy's room seemed to be loose. From there it was but a short step to prising it up, and an even shorter step to discovering Daisy's little pot of goose fat – and a shorter step still to summoning Daisy to the drawing room to receive her punishment.

"What, pray," demanded Miss Gertrude in chilling tones, "is *this*?" And she held up the incriminating pot.

The only reason Daisy was not sent down to the coal cellar was that the coal cellar was full of coal and there wasn't any room. Instead, Miss

Gertrude gave her fifteen strokes on the bottom with a carpet beater. Daisy held on tight to the back of a chair and didn't cry out once.

All the time Miss Gertrude was beating her, the words of the old lady went drumming through her head: *Be strong, my child! The fight is not yet over.*

Daisy *was* strong. But in bed that night, she wept bitterly. She wept for all the sorrows in her life. No mother to love her, no father to protect her. No one in the whole wide world to care what became of her. And now her poor red hands would never be like a lady's!

Daisy was crying so hard into her pillow that she never noticed the attic door open and a shadowy figure steal in. At first, when she turned over and rubbed at her eyes, she thought it was Lottie come to visit her. Lottie had slept in her own bed that night, for Daisy was too sore to cuddle. But it wasn't Lottie. It was the old lady! She was carrying her scrapbook and was showing her legs, all the way from the knee down, just as she had before. It was an extremely strange way for an old lady to dress, but perhaps, thought Daisy, she was a ghost from long ago. People did dress strangely, long ago.

Daisy watched as the old lady settled herself on the chair and opened the scrapbook. Just like last time, she began leafing through it,

pausing every now and again to give her little smile, as if at pleasant memories. Backwards and forwards she went through the book. She came at last to a page near the beginning, and there she paused. Her smile grew pitying, and slowly she shook her white head.

"Poor child! How hard you had to fight!"

Even as the words were said, the attic door was pushed open and another figure came in. This time, it *was* Lottie.

"Daisy!" She blundered across the attic, knocking into the chair as she came. One of her hands passed right through the old lady. "I've been so worried!" Lottie fell with a *flump* on to Daisy's bed. "I couldn't get to sleep and I'm that cold I can't stop shiverin'!"

Daisy peeled the covers back. "You had better get in with me," she said.

By the time Lottie had clambered in and settled herself down, the old lady had gone. If she comes again, vowed Daisy, I am going to be bold and creep up and see what it is that she is looking at!

Chapter five

The months passed, and Daisy had another birthday. Now she was eleven. She felt that it was a great age, yet still her daydreams were no nearer to coming true. Maybe they never would. Maybe she should just give up and be like Lottie. Lottie didn't have ideas above her station. Why should Daisy?

One of the young ladies, a Miss Constance Woodhouse, happened to have a birthday on the same day as Daisy. Constance was eleven, just as Daisy was. But unlike Daisy, Constance had a birthday party and was showered with gifts. Cook laid on a special tea and baked a special cake with snow-white icing and *Happy Birthday, Constance* spelt out in pink sugar roses. Daisy and Lottie crept into the larder to have a look.

"Aow!" breathed Lottie. "Ain't that something?"

"It's beautiful," whispered Daisy. She reached out with a finger, just wanting to feel if the icing really was as crisp and frosty as it looked, but her finger never got there. There was a sharp *whack!* and Daisy went reeling backwards.

"You get away from that cake!" shrieked Cook, raising her ladle to give Daisy another smack.

"Miss Constance don't want you breathin' all over it!"

Daisy ducked, but not quite quickly enough – the ladle caught her on the side of the head and sent her stumbling into the door.

"Serves yer right!" shrilled Cook.

For the rest of the day, Daisy was very subdued. All her sparkle seemed to have deserted her. She crept like a little mouse about her duties, with her eyes cast down and her hair demurely tucked away beneath her cap, the way it was supposed to be (but hardly ever was). Cook breathed heavily through her nostrils and said, "That's better!"

Lottie didn't think it was better. She hated to see Daisy looking so downcast. She tried telling her about the party, to see if it would cheer her up.

"There they was, all sittin' at the table, with Miss Constance at the head, and the cake – aow! The cake!" Lottie rocked, ecstatically. "Like a picture, it was, wiv all its candles a-burnin'. Lor, I wish you could've seen it!"

But Daisy wasn't interested. She didn't care about the cake; she didn't care about the party. She didn't care about anything any more. What was the point of going on pretending? She was never going to get anywhere. It was just a silly daydream. It would never come true!

Daisy threw herself on to her bed and buried her head, as best she could, in the hard pillow.

"Hey!" said Lottie, poking at her.

Daisy made an angry noise into the pillow. "Go away! Leave me alone!"

"But I got you something!"

Reluctantly, Daisy raised her head. "W-what?"

"Got a present."
Lottie plunged
into her pocket
and, with a big,
gap-toothed grin,
pressed something
soft and sticky
into Daisy's hand.
"'Ere y'are! Bit o' cake!"

Lottie had saved it specially for Daisy. She had risked Cook's rage – and Lottie was terribly scared of Cook's rage – to sneak it off a plate as she was clearing the table at the end of the party.

"Oh, but you must have some too!" cried Daisy, trying to push a piece of cake into Lottie's mouth. But Lottie wouldn't.

"I got it for you," she said. "'Cos it's yer birthday."

"Oh, Lottie!" Daisy flung both arms round Lottie's neck. "What would I do without you?"

By next day, Daisy's spirits were back to normal. She was cheeky to Cook, who took a swipe with her ladle (and missed). She sang loudly and cheerfully as she scrubbed the front step.

"I'm o-o-only a *bird* in a *gilded* ca-a-age!"

It was just as well it was Miss Fanny who caught her, and not Miss Gertrude. Miss Fanny said, "Hush, child! Cease that dreadful noise. And put your cap on straight!"

Daisy said, "Yes, ma'am!" and risked a cheeky grin. Miss Fanny shook her head.

"What is to become of you, child? You are too bold by half!"

For their summer show, the young ladies were to put on a display of Greek dancing. They

were having special lessons twice a week in the drawing room. Daisy couldn't resist creeping up to watch! Some of the young ladies – Miss Constance Woodhouse was an example – had to repeat their steps over and over before they could memorise them. Daisy only had to see them once.

At night, in the attic, she showed Lottie what she had learnt.

"And, oh, Lottie!" she giggled. "You should just see some of them, the way they thump about! They are like carthorses."

Lottie giggled too, as Daisy thumped across the attic being a carthorse; but all the same, it scared her.

"There'll be trouble," she said, "if anyone catches yer. Yer know we ain't allowed to watch."

"I know," said Daisy, "but it is such fun!"

The dancing drew her like a magnet. Out in the yard, when she was supposed to be emptying bins, she practised her steps. Cook saw her and walloped her with her ladle and told her to stop showing off.

"T'ain't your place to show off!"

But Daisy couldn't help it. Singing and dancing came as naturally to her as breathing. Not even Cook with her ladle could stop her.

The day of the show came closer, and the young ladies had a final rehearsal, all dressed up in Greek tunics, with sandals on their feet and sprigs of greenery in their hair. Up in the attic, Daisy draped herself in a sheet, stuck a bunch of leaves on her head, kicked off her shoes and danced for Lottie. Lottie stuffed her fist into her mouth. A series of little squeaks came out.

"I don't believe that it's meant to be funny," said Daisy, "but, oh dear! Some of them have such *very* big feet! And some of them—" she couldn't help but giggle, even as she spoke. "Some of them, Lottie, are *knock-kneed*!"

Daisy and Lottie fell together on Daisy's bed, helpless with laughter.

"Knock-kneed!" squealed Lottie.

"Like *this*," said Daisy. And she sprang up and began waddling round the attic like a duck.

"Oh, lor!" Lottie wiped the tears from her eyes. "You'll be the death of me, you will!"

The dancing display was to be held on a Saturday afternoon at the beginning of July. The double doors in the drawing room were opened up, with chairs set at one end for the audience. There was great excitement throughout the school, for a very famous person was going to attend. The famous person was Sir Henry Holby Hunt, who was the uncle of Miss Constance Woodhouse (with the knock-knees) who owned the Jubilee Theatre in the Haymarket. Everyone had heard of the Jubilee Theatre! Even Lottie.

Cook, however, said it was no use Daisy and Lottie working themselves into a froth.

"You'll be down here in the basement, where you belong!"

Cook had plans for keeping them busy the whole afternoon. Try as she might, Daisy wasn't able to sneak away. Cook said, "I've got my eye on you, Miss!" She set Daisy to polishing the silver; and when she had finished that, she sent her on an errand up the road.

Daisy ran like the wind. If she were really quick she might at least be able to escape from Cook for the last few minutes and see the great Sir Henry in the audience. Daisy had never seen a Sir before! Especially not one who owned a theatre.

But she was too late. As she reached the house she heard the sound of clapping, and knew that the display was over. The young ladies would be all lined up, taking their bows. Miss Constance would be wobbling down into her curtsey. Probably toppling over, for she was the clumsiest creature.

Before Daisy knew it, she was prancing across the pavement, being Miss Constance. Simper, simper, prink, prance! Wibble wobble into a most *charming* pose, and then... oops, ouch! Here I go-o-o-o!

All up and down and round about, to and fro across the square danced Daisy. She was still dancing when the doors of the Academy opened and the guests began to leave. Sir Henry came out with a beautiful lady on his arm. The beautiful lady was Madeleine

Belmarsh, a famous actress. She was even more famous than Sir Henry – and Daisy bumped right into her!

"*Oh*, Henry! Look!" Miss Belmarsh caught Daisy by the arm. "Just look! The perfect Dolly!"

Daisy, very red-faced and confused, bobbed down into a curtsey.

"Beggin' yer pardon, ma'am!" She knew better than to speak like a young lady in front of Miss Belmarsh. To speak like a young lady would be considered impertinent. "Beggin' yer pardon, but I'm Daisy, not Dolly."

Miss Belmarsh gave a tinkling laugh. Sir Henry laughed, too. Deep and manly.

"My dear!" said Miss Belmarsh. "Wherever did you learn to dance like that?"

Daisy hung her head. "Taught meself, I did."

"Oh, Henry!" Miss Belmarsh clutched excitedly at Sir Henry's arm. "She *is* perfect, isn't she?" She turned to Daisy. "We are looking for a little girl *just* like you! How would you feel about appearing on stage? Would you be nervous, do you think?"

Daisy's eyes stood out on stalks. *Nervous?* "Not me, ma'am!"

"No?" Miss Belmarsh gave another of her tinkling laughs. "In that case – Henry, give her one of your cards! Come to this address tomorrow morning at eleven o'clock, and we will see what you can do. Can you manage that, do you think?"

Couldn't she just! Daisy nodded so vigorously her cap almost fell off.

"Red hair!" cried Miss Belmarsh, clasping her hands. "How utterly delicious! Henry, we simply *must* have her!"

"Whatever you say, my dear." Gravely, Sir Henry took a card from his pocket and handed it to Daisy. "There! Be careful not to lose it. We shall expect you tomorrow."

Daisy bobbed another curtsey and ran back indoors, clutching her precious card. In her excitement, she ran straight to Miss Gertrude. Surely, now, Miss Gertrude would be pleased with her?

Chapter six

"You *spoke* to her? To Miss *Belmarsh*? You dared to intrude upon her privacy?"

Miss Gertrude's voice quivered and shook. Far from being pleased, she was so extremely angry that little balls of spit came flying from her mouth.

"You actually had the *impertinence* to draw

yourself to her attention?"

Daisy trembled, but stood her ground.

"She said I could go on the stage… she said I were perfect! Beggin' yer pardon, ma'am," added Daisy, remembering her manners.

"You? Go on the stage?" Miss Gertrude flared her nostrils and gave a loud, braying laugh. "Are you out of your mind? An ignorant little thing like you? Why, how would you ever learn your lines? You would not be able to read them!"

I would so! thought Daisy. But she didn't say so for fear of making Miss Gertrude even more angry than she was already.

"I shall not put you down the cellar," said Miss Gertrude. "I shall not even lock you up. I shall simply say this: you set foot outside this house, and that is it. You do not come back. The choice is yours. But be warned!"

Miss Gertrude shot out a bony finger. Daisy jumped backwards in alarm. She thought Miss Gertrude was going to poke her eye out!

"Do not," hissed Miss Gertrude, "seek to throw yourself on *my* mercy when your bubble bursts. You will be out there—" Miss Gertrude flung a dramatic arm in the direction of the street. Her lip curled. "Out there, *crawling in the gutter*, which is where you belong! Now, get out of my sight. You disgust me!"

Daisy turned and ran from the room, almost bumping into Miss Fanny, who was on her knees with her ear to the keyhole.

"Child! Wait!"

Daisy fled for the safety of the back stairs, with Miss Fanny wobbling on little fat legs behind her.

"Oh, Daisy, do be sensible!" she begged.

"Only think how good your life has been since you came to us! A warm bed, a room of your own, all the food you could possibly desire... what can you hope to gain by running away?"

"Miss Belmarsh is going to put me on the stage!" cried Daisy.

Sadly, Miss Fanny shook her head. "You must not believe everything that people tell you, Daisy. Grand ladies like Miss Belmarsh, they take these sudden fancies. But they are just amusing themselves. By this time tomorrow she will have forgotten that you even exist."

"But she *said*!" protested Daisy. "She said I was perfect!"

"Poor child," said Miss Fanny. "My heart bleeds for you! Did I not warn you, right at the start? Be content with your lot! It is the only way you will find happiness."

Lottie, too, begged Daisy to be sensible.

"Just don't do nothin' rash. It ain't worth it!"

"But, oh, Lottie, just think!" Daisy clasped both of Lottie's hands in hers. "This is my big chance! It may never, ever come again!"

"No, an' you won't never be able to come back here again," sobbed Lottie.

"Wouldn't want to!" declared Daisy. They were brave words, but secretly Daisy trembled. Suppose Miss Fanny was right, and by tomorrow Miss Belmarsh had forgotten all about her? Then what would she do? The thought of being on her own was very frightening.

That night, Daisy lay stiff as a board in her narrow bed. Her eyes were hot and aching from all the weeping she had done. Her big chance had come, the chance she had dreamed of for so long ... and was she not to take it?

"Oh, what shall I do?" cried Daisy. "What shall I do?"

A voice spoke in the darkness: "Seize the moment, my child!"

Daisy sprang up in bed. What was that? And then she saw her – the old lady! She was back! Sitting on her chair, going through her scrapbook.

Daisy held her breath. Slowly, slowly, she crept forward up the bed. The old lady gave no sign of being aware of Daisy's presence.

Greatly daring, Daisy peered over the old lady's shoulder. In the scrapbook was a newspaper cutting with a picture of – the old lady! The old lady in a long, beautiful gown, standing on a stage, holding out her hands to an unseen audience. At the top of the page someone had written the word SWANSONG, and the date: 1st May, 1960.

Daisy gave a little gasp. *Nineteen sixty*? Nineteen sixty was the next century! It was decades away! If Daisy lived until 1960 she would be... she counted up on her fingers. She would be *eighty-three*!

What could it mean? Could it mean that the old lady was not from the past but the future? A ghost *from the future*? This was very extraordinary, thought Daisy.

Now the old lady was flicking through the

pages, back to the beginning. Back, back, right to the very start. A smile curved her old, puckered lips. Daisy craned forward, eager to see what she was looking at. It was a theatre programme!

21st July, 1888

Little Dolly Daydream

AT THE JUBILEE THEATRE

Starring
**Miss
MADELEINE BELMARSH**

and
**Mr
FREDERICK CAINE**

Introducing
MARGUERITE MAY
as "Dolly"

Daisy gave a little surprised squeak and clapped a hand over her mouth. Marguerite May! That was her – it was Daisy! The old lady cocked her head, as if, this time, she had heard her. Or maybe it was an echo she had caught, flying across the years. She smiled.

"You fought so hard, little Daisy! So hard to make your dreams come true."

Early next morning, before anyone was up and about, Daisy wrapped her few belongings in her shawl, her precious shawl that she had had from a baby, and tiptoed into Lottie's room.

"Lottie!" Gently, she shook Lottie awake. Lottie's eyes, as she saw the bundle that Daisy was carrying, grew wide and fearful.

"Aow, Daisy! Yer not goin'?"

"I have to," said Daisy. "It is my big chance.

But Lottie, I shall come back for you! Just as soon as I am famous. That is a *promise*."

In later years, Daisy often thought back to those long-ago days when she had still been plain little Daisy May, beaten by Miss Gertrude, smacked by Cook, living upstairs in the attic. As an old, old lady, she would sit by the fire and leaf through her scrapbook and smile as she remembered. And faithful Lottie would doze by her side, for Daisy – or Marguerite, as she became – had kept her promise.

"It all came true, you see, Lottie! Just as I told you."

Dreams *can* come true, if you believe in them hard enough.